For May and Conan - AH
For Kylie - NS

First published in 2020 by
Scholastic Children's Books
Euston House, 24 Eversholt Street,
London NW1 1DB
a division of Scholastic Ltd

PB ISBN: 978 1 407191 44 7
C&F PB ISBN: 978 0 702303 46 3
HB ISBN: 978 0 702303 20 3

London   New York   Toronto   Sydney   Auckland
Mexico City   New Delhi   Hong Kong
www.scholastic.co.uk

LETTERS

10 9 8 7 6 5 4
Text © Alice Hemming, 2020
Illustrations © Nicola Slater, 2020
The moral rights of Alice Hemming and Nicola Slater
have been asserted.

FSC
www.fsc.org
MIX
Paper from
responsible sources
FSC® C008047

the LEAF THIEF

Alice Hemming

Nicola Slater

SCHOLASTIC

"What a **wonderful** time of year!
I am snug in my nest with a belly full of hazelnuts
and the sun is shining through my leafy canopy.
Such lovely colours:

red, gold, orange . . .

red, gold, orange . . .

"Your . . . leaf?"

"Yes. One of my leaves is MISSING. My leaf looked a lot like that one. The one Mouse has got."

"That is not your leaf, Squirrel."

"But how can you be sure? Mouse? Mouse! Did you steal my leaf?"

"No.
This is my
boat."

"See, Squirrel?
It is perfectly normal to lose
a leaf or two at this time of
year... OK?"

"OK, thanks, Bird.
See you tomorrow."

This happened last year, remember?

Maybe.

Why don't you go back to your nest and try to relax?

OK, thanks, Bird.

"Try to relax . . .

breathe in . . . and out . . .

Just relax . . . "

The following morning...

This is a DISASTER!

Bird?

BIRD!

WHERE ARE YOU, BIRD?

"I'm here, Squirrel."

"No, Squirrel.
I am not the Leaf Thief.
I will SHOW you the
Leaf Thief."

"Where are they?
Because I've got a few things
I'd like to say to them!"

"Look around you.
The **Leaf Thief** is everywhere.

It shakes the trees . . .

and rustles the leaves . . .

it even takes people's hats!

Do you see the Leaf Thief, Squirrel?"

"The only thief is the **WIND**!
This happens every year in the autumn. Every year!
The leaves fade and the wind blows them away.
They'll grow back again in the spring.
Now, I'm going home. Please don't disturb me again."

"It was just the wind.
The leaves fade and the wind blows them away.
Of course! No Leaf Thief at all. Silly me.
I'm going to sleep well tonight!"

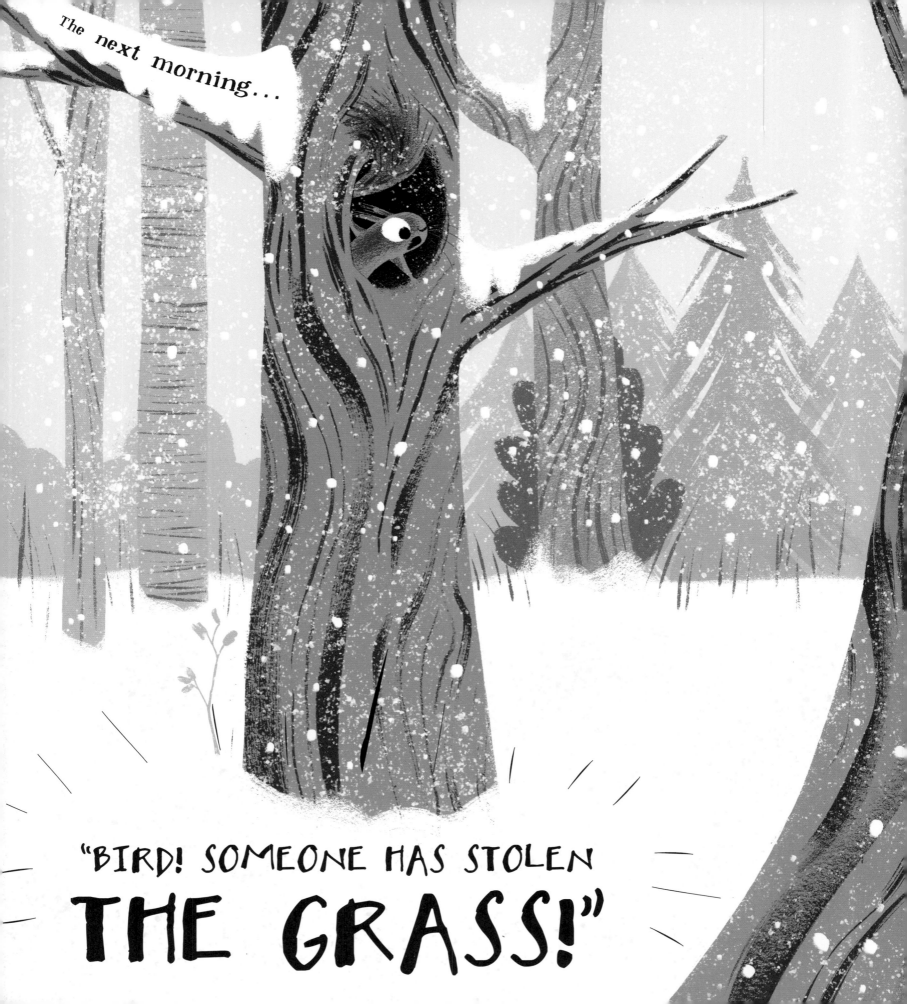

The real Leaf Thief

As squirrel found out, nobody is really stealing
the leaves from the trees.

Bird says,
"The only thief is the WIND"

But there is more to it than that. The wind can
only blow the leaves away when the trees have
started to shed their leaves. This happens in the
autumn when the temperature drops, marking
the change from summer to winter.

Trees look very pretty in the autumn

Before the leaves fall, they turn from green to
all sorts of different colours.

"red, gold, orange"

When they turn brown, the leaves are dead and
ready to fall from the tree.

Not all trees shed their leaves

Only deciduous trees lose their leaves. Evergreens keep theirs.

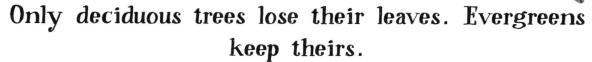

Autumn happens at different times across the world

In the Northern Hemisphere, autumn starts in September. In the Southern Hemisphere, it starts in March.

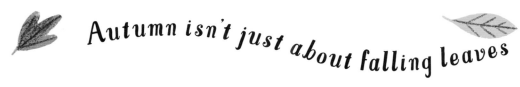

Autumn isn't just about falling leaves

Other changes happen too. The daylight hours shorten and some birds and butterflies fly to warmer countries, or migrate. Other animals, like bats and hedgehogs hibernate.

Squirrels don't hibernate but they do store nuts and other food for the colder months ahead. They also begin to sleep a lot more.